Tugboats Never Sleep

Tugboats Never Sleep

by
Kathryn Lasky

Photographs by
Christopher G. Knight

Little, Brown and Company
BOSTON   TORONTO

Also by Kathryn Lasky and Christopher G. Knight
I HAVE FOUR NAMES FOR MY GRANDFATHER

We wish to thank the Boston Tow Boat Company,
the men of the *Cabot,* and Jason and his family
for making this book possible.

K.L./C.K.

FIRST EDITION

T 09/77

Library of Congress Cataloging in Publication Data

Lasky, Kathryn.
   Tugboats never sleep.

   SUMMARY: A little boy spends a morning on a tugboat and later dreams of the day when he too may be
a deckhand.
   [1. Tugboats — Fiction] I. Knight, Christopher G. II. Title.
PZ7.L3274Tu   [E]   77-4651
ISBN 0-316-51518-3

*Published simultaneously in Canada
by Little, Brown & Company (Canada) Limited*

PRINTED IN THE UNITED STATES OF AMERICA

To my parents

I see their lights—
orange, green and white on the night water
floating like Christmas trees in the blackness.

Everyone thinks I am asleep, but I'm not.
In my loft high above the city
I am a night watcher.
And on a starry night there is nothing better
than to stay up late and watch the tugboats
in Boston Harbor from the window by my bed.

The tugboats never sleep.
There is always some big ship from far away that needs
a push and a tug into the harbor and up Chelsea Creek.

It might be the *Prince of Fundy* from Nova Scotia
or the *Gothic Lady* from England or the *Gulf Tiger*
from Louisiana — names that taste like dreams.

And when the tugs push and pull, I can hear their code of
whistles right in my bed high above Boston Harbor.

One toot says "start pushing."
Two toots say "pull back."
Three toots say "job finished."

I fall asleep with the sound in my ears.

I wake up. Saturday!
I'm on my way.
Tug *Walton*, Tug *Triton*,
Tug *Mars* and Tug *Cabot*,
here I come.

Quickly, down the ladder from my loft bed,
down forty-five steps of stairs
to the sidewalk,

down North Street,
then Prince . . .

through a street of green cabbages, red onions, flowers and tomatoes,
past a window with ten thousand cookies,
past four rabbits hanging upside down,
past an old lady dressed all in black,
who says, "God bless you child,"
past a fat baby in a silly little hat,

past a noodle factory
and the Mariners House,
where old sailors play checkers,
past a hidden garden on Fleet Street.
Then at the corner where Moon meets Sun
I get a pain in my side.
So I catch my breath.

But I can see the big T,
and I can smell the baked beans from here.

One block more and—
"I'm here!" I shout. "May I come aboard?"

"Aye, Mate Jason, just in time for morning dinner,
must be Saturday."

He is the real mate, not me.
His name is Arvard Tristam McGray,
but everybody calls him "Tut" for short.

"Come aboard."

And as soon as I climb on board the Tug *Cabot,*
cook sticks his head out a porthole and rings
a bell—dinner time!

On tugboats they call lunch dinner
and eat it at breakfast time.

Chowder, turkey, baked beans, green beans,
mashed potatoes, chocolate cake—that's what you eat
for dinner at breakfast time on a tug.

I sit at the table with Captain Forbes
and Kelsey, the engine man, and John, the oiler
for the engines, and Jimmy, the deckhand.

They tell big stories about the time a ship as big as an island came into Boston Harbor and nearly got stuck in Chelsea Creek, but the tugs saved her.

And they tell little stories—about how John, the oiler, got the Kewpie doll tattoo on his arm.

But Jimmy tells the best stories of all.
He tells me about pulling up to a five-hundred-foot ship
and throwing the heaving rope that ends in a knot called
a monkey's fist. He throws it straight up to a deckhand
who doesn't speak English. And then he has to run really fast
to the other end of the tug and throw another heaving rope
to another deckhand who doesn't speak English either.

So they talk in "rope," and they know exactly
what each other means.
They know how to throw them and catch them—back and
forth between two moving boats.
They know when to tie the big ship and the little tug
together . . . and how tight and when to let up.

Today Jimmy shows me some important rope talk.
How to make a clove hitch knot.
"Hold this rope, Jason. Now watch me and do the same."
Jimmy doesn't say another word.
He makes two loops with his rope.
Then I make two loops with mine.

He puts the first loop on top of the second one.
I put the first loop on top of the second one.
He slips his over a deck post; I put mine over another rope.
He pulls his tight.
I pull mine tight.

"You did it Jason."
"I did it! I made a clove hitch!"

"Got to fetch the *Hellenic Sky*. Better run home now, Jason."
Says Tut.
"O.K. Thanks for dinner."
"Aye, Mate."

Someday I'll be old enough to go and throw the ropes with
Jimmy and help the biggest ships in the world come into Boston Harbor.
"Hey, Jason," Jimmy shouts out over the engines as they pull
away. "Be here tomorrow morning. You can tie us up with the
clove hitch. I'll throw you a rope."
"You mean it, Jimmy?"
But the engines roared and he didn't hear me.

By the time I get to the top of the hill
I can't see Jimmy or Tut or Captain Forbes or John, the oiler,
or cook, but I can see Tug *Cabot* nuzzling up to the big cargo
ship like a puppy against an elephant.
And slowly the *Hellenic Sky* starts to swing around.

All afternoon I think about the tugs and practice my knots. And that night on the ladder to my loft bed, I tie a clove hitch and think about the tugs.

I think about a long time ago when only tall
sailing ships came to Boston Harbor.
Even then, when they lowered their sails the little tugs
were there to help push the tall ones through the harbor.

I dream one thousand sailing ships come to Boston and I
speak rope with deckhands from Finland and Spain and Halifax . . .
I throw ropes and never miss.
And I run up and down the tug deck fixing the lines between
me and the tall ships.
I tie clove hitches, the ones Jimmy taught me, making them
tighter and then looser as the little tug pushes the sailing
ships around.

I am the deckhand on the tugboat that brings in
all the great sailing ships to Boston . . .
Maruffa — I am there with my ropes,
Black Pearl . . . Esmeralda . . . Regina Maris . . . Westward . . .
Jason, deckhand of the *Cabot* is there.

The northwest wind blows my ears full of soft whistles.
The sun is not up yet.
But the tugboats never sleep.
In my loft bed high above the city, in the early morning
light I can see the Tug *Cabot* pushing a ship as big as
an island into the harbor, up toward Chelsea Creek.
Today is the day of the clove hitch.
When I hear the three toots I'll be off.
Between the moon and the sun, in the earliest light of
the day there is nothing better than waiting on a pier
to catch a rope from Jimmy on the tug.